This LITTLE MAMMOTH belongs to

_____

_____

_____

First published in Great Britain 1989
by William Heinemann Ltd
First United States edition published 1989
by Philomel Books, a division of The Putnam & Grosset Group
Published 1991 by Little Mammoth
an imprint of Mandarin Paperbacks
Michelin House, 81 Fulham Road, London SW3 6RB

Mandarin is an imprint of the Octopus Publishing Group

Text copyright © 1989 by Patricia Lee Gauch
Illustrations copyright © 1989 by Satomi Ichikawa

ISBN 0 7497 0596 5

A CIP catalogue record for this title
is available from the British Library

Printed in Great Britain by Scotprint Ltd., Musselburgh.

SATOMI ICHIKAWA

Tanya loved to dance

Text by Patricia Lee Gauch

LITTLE
MAMMOTH

For Claudine and Anne
who love dance

Little Tanya loved to dance.

When her elder sister Elise put on her leotard and slippers to practise, Tanya put on her shirt and took off her shoes to practise too.

When Elise did her positions – first, second, fourth and fifth, Tanya did too.

When Elise did a perfect *plié*, Tanya did too.

When Elise practised her *pirouette* and *arabesque*, Tanya did the same.
Tanya particularly liked to do the arabesque.

Sometimes Tanya liked to dance alone,

or dance a *pas de deux* with her ballerina bear Barbara.

And when her mother put on *Swan Lake,* and Elise danced a whole song in arabesques and *jetés* right across the living room floor, Tanya put on her tutu and danced arabesques and jetés across the living room floor too. Tanya made a very good sad swan.

But when Elise went to her lesson, and
Tanya wanted to go too, her mother said,
"You're too little, Tanya. Someday..."

And so sometimes Tanya would go along but only to watch her sister Elise and all of the other dancers through the big window, as they danced their arabesques and their jetés across the wide dance floor.

One day, when it was spring and the flowers were opening their eyes,
Elise got ready for a special dancing display.

She put on a new tutu with petals, and pink lipstick which she was never to use, and a dab of rouge on each cheek, and her mother combed her hair into a long, beautiful silky plait.

And everybody came to see Elise dance. Grandma and Grandpa from the country came. Aunt May who always wore a hat, and Uncle Ernie who never smiled came.

And Tanya came and tried to see over the man with the lumpy hat who sat right in front of her. By sitting on her feet, Tanya could see that Elise was a wonderful flower, doing her arabesques and her pliés just right.

And soon Tanya was very happy and sleepy as well.

"You have a dancer in your family," Aunt May whispered as the family left the large room with all of the hats and voices. Tanya did not even hear for she was fast asleep in her mother's arms.

But when they all got home and drank coffee and laughed and said what a good dancer Elise was, someone put on *Swan Lake* and Tanya woke up.

And while nobody was looking, Tanya found her tutu, and her scarf.
And Tanya danced too all alone.

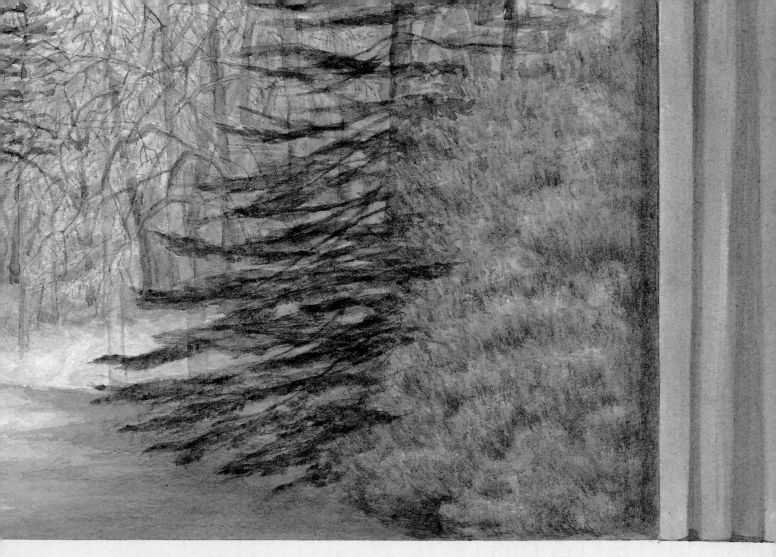

The music played loud and sweet, and she did a plié and arabesque
and five grands jetés right across the floor.

"Dance, Tanya," her sister said, and her mother held her breath. Grandma looked over her glasses. "You have two dancers in your family," she said. Everyone in the room clapped. Elise did too.

Tanya was such a wonderful sad swan.

"A bow, Tanya," her mother said, and Tanya bowed.

Then she crawled back up onto her mother's lap, like a tired kitten,
and went to sleep again.

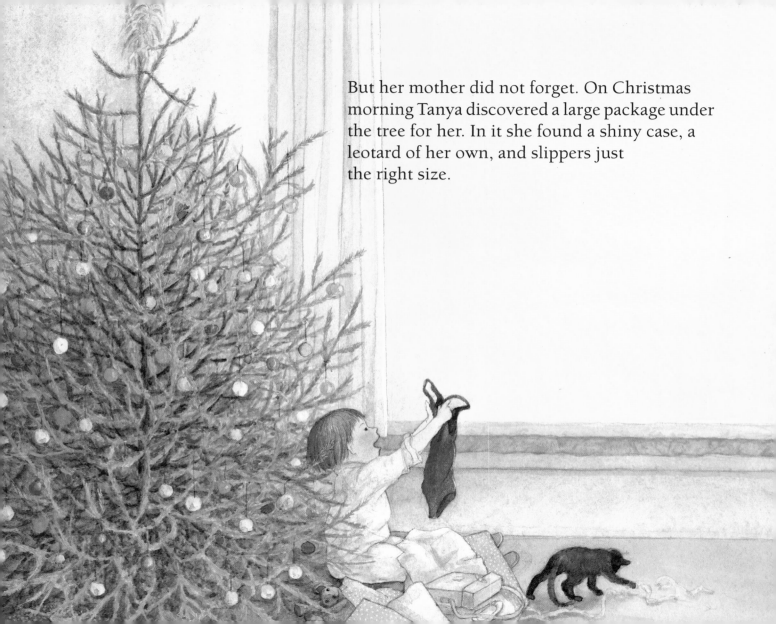

But her mother did not forget. On Christmas
morning Tanya discovered a large package under
the tree for her. In it she found a shiny case, a
leotard of her own, and slippers just
the right size.

"Come along, Tanya," her mother said when it was time to go to Elise's lesson. "Bring your case," her sister said, and Tanya knew she wasn't too little anymore.